THE WILD, WILD INSIDE

A View from Mommy's Tummy!

Kate Feiffer

ILLUSTRATED BY
Laura Huliska-Beith

A PAULA WISEMAN BOOK

SIMON & SCHUSTER BOOKS FOR YOUNG READERS · NEW YORK   LONDON   TORONTO   SYDNEY

Hello.

I know what my name will be.

My parents don't know yet.
They think my name might be Molly.
But they also think it might be James.
The problem is, they don't know if I'm a boy or a girl.
That's because I'm still in my mom's tummy.

At first they said that if I
was a girl, they wanted to
name me Cynthia.

Then they changed
their minds and decided
to name me Jasmine.

Then they changed
their minds and decided
to name me Sheila.

Then they changed their minds
and decided to name me Molly.

My parents change
their minds a lot.

Here are all the boy names
they wanted to name me before
they decided on James:

People always ask my mom,

"What's the baby doing?"

She always tells them the same thing.
She says, "The baby's sleeping," or
"The baby's eating," or "The baby's kicking."
Sure, I do those things. But that's
not all I do.
There are a lot of other
things that I do that she
never mentions.

Take this morning. My mom was in the shower and my sister, Emily, came into the bathroom to ask her,

"What's the baby doing?"

My mom told her, "The baby's sleeping."

I wasn't sleeping, though.
I was on a boat.

I was on a boat in the ocean in a
big storm. A big, HUGE, GIGANTIC
rainstorm. I definitely wasn't sleeping!

Later, when my mom picked my
brother, Gus, up at school, he got in
the car and asked her,

"What's the baby doing?"

As she drove off, she told him,
"The baby's eating."

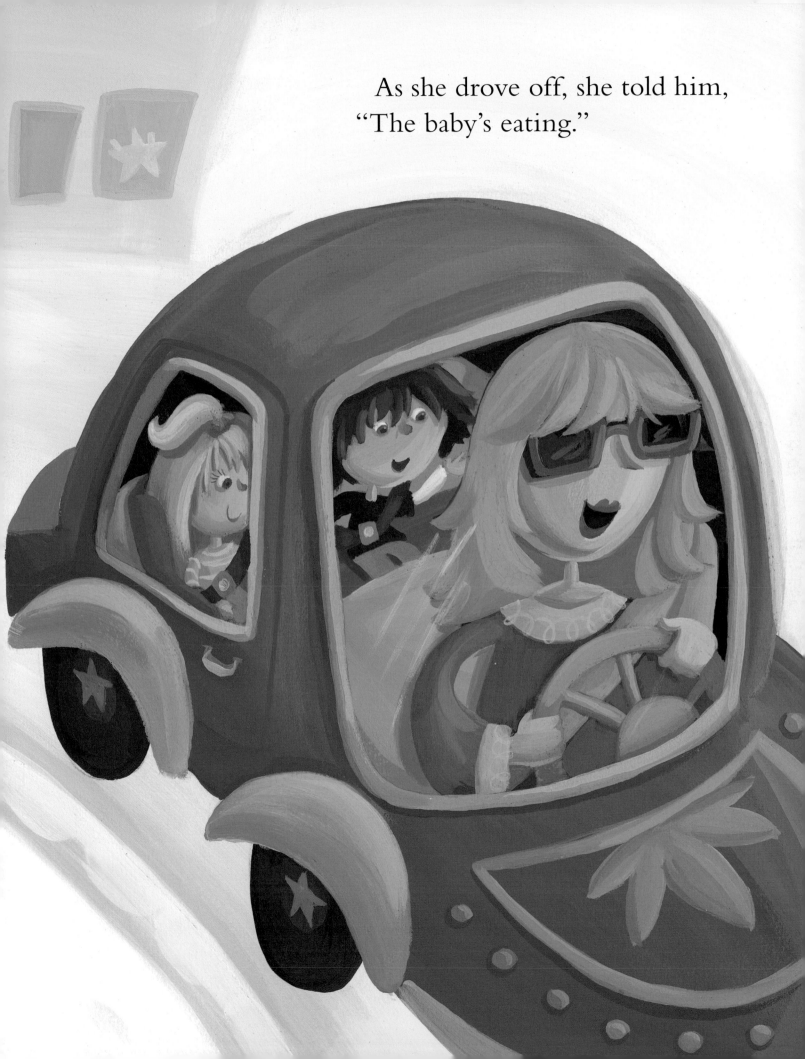

But I wasn't eating. I was in a rocket ship flying two hundred miles above the earth. I was on my way to the moon. And I was making good time, too. I passed a lot of other rocket ships along the way. That is, until I got stuck in a rocket ship traffic jam.

When my mom and dad were making dinner,
my sister, Emily, asked my mom,

"What's the baby doing?"

My mom said,
"The baby's sleeping."

But my mom was wrong again. I was preparing a feast for hundreds—hundreds of HUNGRY dogs. AND I HAD TO COOK FAST.

After dinner my mom, my dad, Emily,
and Gus were dancing, and my dad asked,

"What's the baby doing?"

And my mom said, "The baby's kicking."

I wasn't kicking. I was dancing too. I'm a ballerina and I was leaping across a stage.

When my mom was reading Emily and Gus
a good-night story and they asked,

"What's the baby doing?"

she said, "The baby's sleeping."

This time she was almost right. I was doing yoga.
It had been a busy day and I needed to relax.

But when my grandma called and asked,

"What's the baby doing?"

and my mom said,
"The baby's eating,"

. . . I wasn't eating. How can you eat when you are playing baseball? I had just hit a home run and was sliding into home plate.

In the middle of the night when my mom couldn't sleep and woke up my dad and he asked,

"What's the baby doing?"

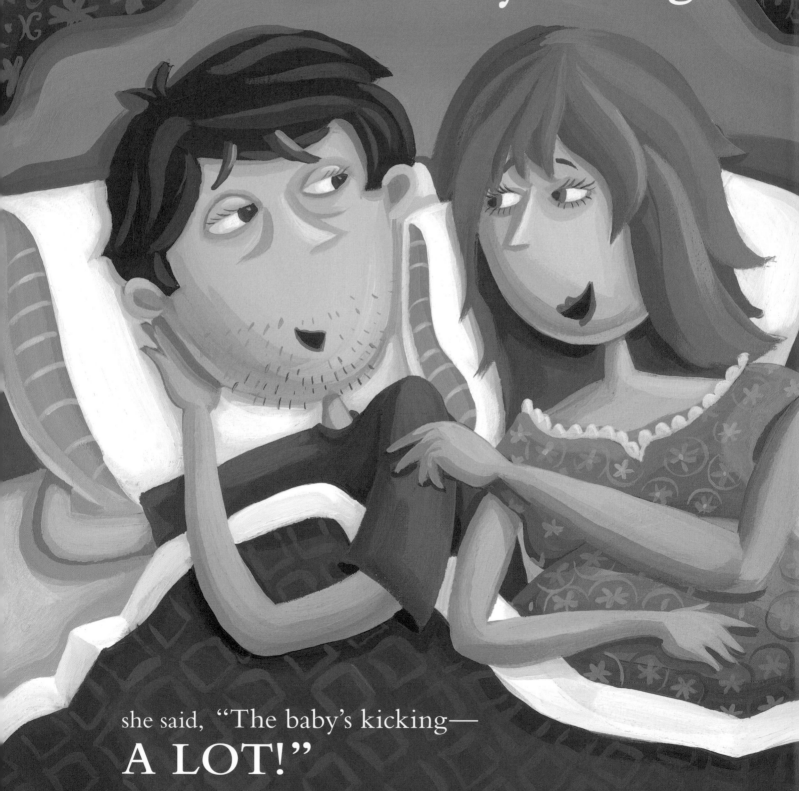

she said, "The baby's kicking—
A LOT!"

This time I wasn't
sailing through a storm.

And I wasn't on my way
to the moon.

And I wasn't feeding
hundreds of hungry dogs
or leaping across a stage.

I wasn't doing yoga or
playing baseball either.

No, I'm not doing any of that right now.
But I am very, very busy. In fact, I am busier than
I've been all day.
My mom says, "It's time. The baby wants to be born."
This time she is right.

That's exactly what I am doing.

Hello,
Molly!

Real-Life Stories

WHAT WERE *YOU* DOING IN *YOUR* MOM'S TUMMY?

"I was playing in your tummy and singing and dancing. I could bounce around on my head."
Finn, AGE 4

"I was surfing and hula dancing, and my head would shake and my feet would kick."
Mina, AGE 5

Ruby: "I was playing tennis with my sister. Klara was building our clubhouse."
Klara: "It was like being inside a disco ball."
Ruby and Klara, TWINS, AGE 6

"I went into a jungle and I saw lots of animals."
Jonas, AGE 5

"I played patty-cake and sang songs."
Drew, AGE 2

"When I was stuck in your belly, I used to paint with my fingers."
Alexa, AGE 5

"It was snuggly in your tummy. I had a crib and a horse and a lamb and a lion.
It was pinkish-purple and snuggly."
Madeline, AGE 7

For Pat and Kerry—K. F.

For Jackson, Cameron, and Baby Claire . . .
the newest wild and wonderful additions to the family!—L. B. H.

SIMON & SCHUSTER BOOKS FOR YOUNG READERS • An imprint of Simon & Schuster Children's Publishing Division • 1230 Avenue of the Americas, New York, New York 10020 • Text copyright © 2010 by Kate Feiffer • Illustrations copyright © 2010 by Laura Huliska-Beith • All rights reserved, including the right of reproduction in whole or in part in any form. • SIMON & SCHUSTER BOOKS FOR YOUNG READERS is a trademark of Simon & Schuster, Inc. • For information about special discounts for bulk purchases, please contact Simon & Schuster Special Sales at 1-866-506-1949 or business@simonandschuster.com. • The Simon & Schuster Speakers Bureau can bring authors to your live event. For more information or to book an event, contact the Simon & Schuster Speakers Bureau at 1-866-248-3049 or visit our website at www.simonspeakers.com. • Book design by Jessica Handelman • The text for this book is set in Bembo. • The illustrations for this book are rendered in acrylic paint. • Manufactured in China • 10 9 8 7 6 5 4 3 2 • Library of Congress Cataloging-in-Publication Data • Feiffer, Kate. • The wild, wild inside : a view from Mommy's tummy! / Kate Feiffer ; illustrated by Laura Huliska-Beith.—1st ed. • p. cm. • "A Paula Wiseman Book." • Summary: An about-to-be-born baby girl describes some of the things she does inside her mother's belly, like yoga, ballet dancing, playing baseball, and cooking a feast for hundreds of hungry dogs. • ISBN: 978-1-4169-4099-9 (hardcover) • [1. Pregnancy—Fiction. 2. Childbirth—Fiction. 3. Babies—Fiction. 4. Family life—Fiction. 5. Humorous stories.] I. Huliska-Beith, Laura, 1964– ill. II. Title. • PZ7.F33346Wi 2010 [E]—dc22 • 2008052270 • 0110 SCP